The City
of Ink
Drinkers

The City of Ink Drinkers

story by ÉRIC SANVOISIN
illustrations by MARTIN MATJE

LA CITÉ DES BUVEURS D'ENCRE
translated by GEORGES MOROZ

Delacorte Press

For Nathan, alias our little #6

Published by
Delacorte Press
an imprint of
Random House Children's Books
a division of Random House, Inc.
1540 Broadway
New York, New York 10036

First American Edition 2002
Originally published by Les Éditions Nathan, Paris, 2001

Visit us on the Web! www.randomhouse.com/kids
Educators and librarians, for a variety of teaching tools, visit us at
www.randomhouse.com/teachers

Library of Congress Cataloging-in-Publication Data

Sanvoisin, Eric.
[Cité des buveurs d'encre. English]
The city of ink drinkers = La cité des buveurs d'encre / story by Eric Sanvoisin ;
illustrations by Martin Matje ; translated by Georges Moroz.
p. cm.
Summary: An ink-drinking vampire and his young fellow book-suckers must pull up stakes and find a new home when subway tunnels threaten to collapse their cemetery.
ISBN 0-385-72972-3
[1. Vampires—Fiction. 2. Books and reading—Fiction. 3. Humorous stories.]   I. Title:
Cité des buveurs d'encre. II. Matje, Martin, ill. III. Moroz, Georges. IV. Title.
PZ7.S238635 Ci 2002
[Fic]—dc21

2001047179

The text of this book is set in 15-point Goudy.
Manufactured in the United States of America
February 2002
10 9 8 7 6 5 4 3 2 1

The City of Ink Drinkers

one

Cheese Holes in the Cemetery

Carmilla and I were quietly drinking a book with our twin straw when Draculink unexpectedly stormed into our dining vault. "A true disaster, kids!" he growled. Then he collapsed into his casket, a worn-out antique that crashed with a thunderous noise.

"Are you okay, Uncle?" Carmilla asked with a loving smile.

Stuck between the broken planks and the coffin's support, Draculink was cursing like the devil. "Well, at least I am in one piece!" he muttered, dusting himself off.

This reminded me of my first encounter with the old ink drinker. I had been trying to escape from him and had unwittingly caused his casket to fall.

In those days, I hated reading. And because I was the son of a bookseller, I was an embarrassment to the whole family. But thanks to a fateful bite of Draculink's razor-sharp, nib-shaped teeth, I forever acquired a taste for ink.

Now, just as he does, I drink books with a straw. I slurp stories,

2

sentence after sentence, like a glutton. It's quite a treat! As the sentences flow through my mouth, they tickle the tip of my tongue. I get to taste all sorts of adventures. Too bad if the pages turn white after being sipped!

One day I am an Indian at war against the white men. The next I'm a caveman, waging fierce battle against fearsome saber-toothed beasts. Draculink has truly made life quite interesting. . . .

An odd noise suddenly brought me back to the present situation. It was Uncle. He was attempting to work his way out of his awkward position. Once he stood up, he burst out laughing, a deep, hollow laugh. I started wondering if he was going bonkers as a result of the fall on his head.

"Something wrong, Uncle?" I asked.

His laughter went on a leave of absence.

"I'm so-so, my dear Odilon. Although, now that my casket is dismantled, the move will be much easier. . . ."

"The move!" Carmilla exclaimed with disbelief. "We're moving?"

Draculink looked at us with his customary grim expression. "This is the very disaster I was about to announce to the two of you," he said.

"But why on earth is this happening?" Carmilla and I shouted together.

"Just follow me, I've got something to show you."

Our guide was floating four inches above the ground. He led us through the network of ever-wider paths until we reached the entrance of the cemetery. There, on the large

and rusty main gate, hung a notice bearing
the town logo:

TO ALL TOWNSPEOPLE!

FOR SAFETY REASONS, THE CEMETERY

WILL BE MOVED TO A NEW LOCATION

NEXT MONTH.

THANK YOU FOR YOUR UNDERSTANDING.

THE MAYOR

"You were right, Uncle. This is a
genuine disaster," muttered Carmilla.
Her hand, lodged in mine, felt like
an ice cube.

Draculink started a round of
explanations in his school-
teacher tone.

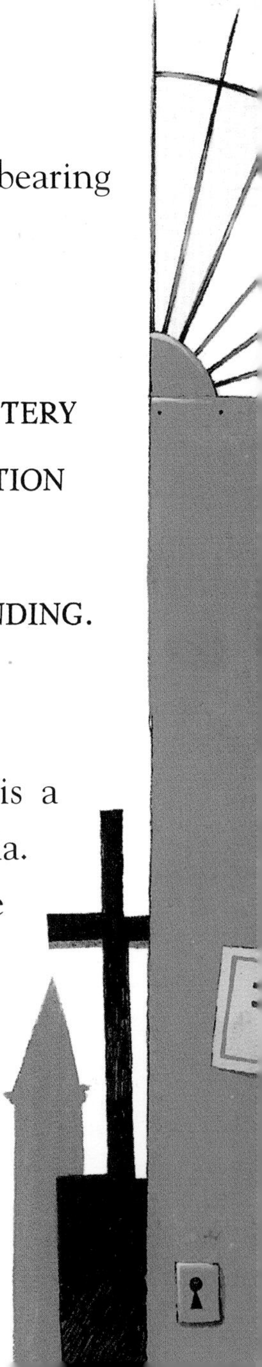

5

"There is a subway line running just under our cemetery," he began. "A real Swiss cheese! Soon the whole thing will crash. You can imagine the headlines in the newspapers: *The Dead Are Haunting the Corridors of the Subway!* So, kids, we too are packing."

What a mess! All my plans were wrecked! For the time being, I was still living at my parents', just above the bookstore, and visiting Carmilla on Wednesdays and weekends. But my dream was to marry her and live with her in the cemetery. Ever since I became Carmilla's boyfriend, books have been tasting even better! With a twin straw, we slurp the little bookies as a duo. Ink flows through our straw at an average speed of ten words per second. That Carmilla, she's the ink drinker of my life.

At night, I sometimes dream that I'm the daddy of tiny ink suckers, and I see myself making a straw for three, for four, for five. . . .

But the coming move was smashing my dreams to pieces.

two

What's Your Great Idea, Genius?

A move, but where to and for how long? I started pacing about in our dining vault, as restless as a goldfish in its tank. Carmilla couldn't stop staring at me.

"Things look very bad, kids."

Draculink was back from a visit to the new cemetery. Sadly, the place was too small and without vaults. In addition to the three of us, thousands of books were sitting in storage. We needed some truly spacious quarters.

"I'm sure you have a solution, Uncle," I said hopefully.

The ink drinker cleared his throat without looking at me directly.

"Well, I thought we could move into your father's bookstore temporarily, until we find a better spot."

I saw my face change color in the mirror that stood atop Carmilla's dresser: I was turning purple, the very color of ink exposed too long to the sun.

"But that's nuts! Three caskets in a bookstore . . ."

"Isn't there a cellar under the shop?"

"Yes, but it's tiny. And don't forget, Uncle, my dad keeps a close eye on his inventory. If he finds a book that doesn't belong, he'll smell a rat. How will we conceal our huge food reserve?"

Draculink frowned, drawing his thick eyebrows together.

"Well, we might consider leaving our fodder here and drinking your father's books."

I went into a rage as dark as the ink we were talking about.

"It's a crime! If you touch a single page of my father's book-ies, the poor man will die!"

Seeing how resolute I was, Draculink backed down.

"I was just kidding, Odilon. I am an old and weary ink drinker. Truth is, I don't have a clue about what to do. But time is running out and we've got to find a solution before tomorrow."

The situation was dire.

"How about moving into a local public library?" said Carmilla. "It would be bigger and we'd be less conspicuous than in a bookstore."

"Nonsense, Carmilla! It's too crowded in a public space," I said. "Our presence would be quickly noticed. What we need is a library with millions of books and hundreds of storage rooms. The problem is there's no such place in town."

12

"Since you're so clever, find a solution and we'll implement it!"

I looked at her with a seductive smile. "I happen to have one."

"So, what's your great idea, genius? What is your miraculous thought?"

I remained silent for a few seconds, the better to relish my triumphant victory.

"Let's change cemeteries."

Carmilla giggled. I felt she was about to make mincemeat of my idea.

"It's clear you're an inexperienced and half-baked ink drinker. Otherwise, you'd know that old vampires like Uncle

Draculink can't be more than a mile away from their cemetery of origin or they dry up into dust."

"But that doesn't apply to you and me," I replied.

"You're not thinking of abandoning Uncle, are you?"

I was in such a state of uncontrollable anger that I nearly answered, "Why not?" Instead, I left the vault and slammed the gate. I needed fresh air to think more clearly. On my way out, I heard Carmilla shout:

"If we don't find a solution by tonight, I'll have to go back to my parents' place! Is that what you want?"

I felt overwhelmed with sadness. Carmilla was staying at her uncle's to study, since her family inhabited a very remote cemetery in the middle of mountains. My father would never allow me to travel hundreds of miles to be with Carmilla. And what would happen to dear old Uncle Draculink?

I exited the cemetery with dark and gloomy thoughts. I didn't know where my feet were leading me. And then I started to daydream. . . .

three

Ink Under the Bridges

I was walking along the piers of the Chapter River, which splits our city into two parts. Contemplating the flow of the water was somewhat comforting. I imagined a river of ink flowing out of a colossal library. The words from thousands of novels poured out at my feet and I only had to bend down to grab them.

I wondered: How would it feel to drink several books at the same time? I knew about sharing a book with another person. But absorbing two books simultaneously, a sentence from one and a paragraph from another, might very well be pleasurable.

I found the idea so thrilling that I started dancing in the streets.

It was like a double allowance of adventure, fear, joy, and laughter! Start as a horseback-riding cowboy, then become an astronaut aboard a rocket. Flee in front of Indians, then catch a fearsome extraterrestrial! And how about mixing stories? Live under a tent lost in the cosmos, or attack a stagecoach with a laser gun . . .

Very simple! Just use the twin straw in reverse mode!

All these thoughts made me dizzy. I was tempted to dive into the river's fresh ink, so as to drink and quench my thirst.

And then the dream vanished. The Chapter River turned back into water. Anger welled up again in my mind. Those blasted ink drinkers had caused so much trouble in my life. I had been innocent until that fateful day when Draculink showed up in my father's bookstore. Until then, I thought a straw was merely used to sip lemonade. . . .

Out of anger, I kicked a pebble. I was tracking its path with my eyes when I had a flabbergasting vision: An immense tower—higher than the Eiffel Tower, taller than the twin towers of the World Trade Center—assumed the shape of an open book. . . . It was amazing! I'd never seen it before. The tower had sprung out of nowhere.

The magical appearance of the gigantic building erased my anger. Could this be a sign sent by the god of the ink drinkers himself?

four

A Casket Too Small for a Mummy

As I returned to the cemetery, night was falling. A furious Carmilla rushed toward me.

"Where have you been? I thought you had abandoned us. That you didn't like me anymore!"

23

She went on without letting me reply.

"Do you realize that we have one night left to move and we don't even know where to go? You should see how poorly Uncle Draculink is doing!"

I went down into the vault to assess the damage. Lying down in Carmilla's casket, his arms and legs overflowing the edges, Draculink seemed to have dried up. I touched his cheeks. They felt like old, decaying paper.

Suddenly I got scared; he was motionless, much like a mummy.

"Uncle Draculink!" I shook his inanimate body, eliciting merely a sound of crumpled paper.

Carmilla came up behind me. Her silence was as chilling as a

24

death sentence. I knew what she was thinking deep down: The awful state of Draculink and the fact that we were at a loss about where to go were all my fault!

How wrong she was!

I bent down toward the ink drinker and muttered a few words in his ear. Something secret . . .

Draculink opened an eye that looked as if it had been tinted with red ink. But in the blue of his iris, I saw that he was coming back to life. He smoothed out his crumpled cheeks with the palms of his hands, licked his transparent lips with the sharp tip of his tongue, and clumsily sat up in his niece's casket. The wood creaked, while his bones crackled.

"Quite interesting, my boy!"

Then Draculink jumped out of the casket, as nimble as a young man. Thanks to me, his zest for life was back!

"Wait a minute!" Carmilla shouted. Her cheeks were on fire, and her wavy hair slithered like a nest of snakes. "The two of you aren't going to get away with that! I hate hushed conversations."

Given the way she had welcomed me earlier, I was eager to get even.

"Uncle Draculink, do you think we can trust her?" I teased.

The old ink drinker quietly rubbed his chin.

"I don't know, dear Odilon. She is not her usual self. I leave it up to you to decide."

"Oh, I hate you both!"

Carmilla rushed at me. I was able to dodge her scratching fingernails and grab her wrists.

She was so mad that her name—which was carved on my arm—was burning my skin.

"Carmilla, my sweet other half, we are leaving this place forever. I found a treasure this afternoon: The giant library I was dreaming of is almost next door."

five

I Have a Story to Tell You

We packed the pieces of Draculink's casket into Carmilla's and put the whole thing on top of mine. With the ink drinker at one end and Carmilla and me at the other, off we went, in small steps, toward our new dwelling.

As we got closer, my excitement was building and words were gushing out of my mouth.

"It's a giant library called the Library of the World," I said.

"How beautiful!" said Carmilla as she admired the glass walls, which were brilliantly shining under the full moon.

"Uncle Draculink," I went on, "do you realize that this place has hundreds of rooms, and nooks and crannies for us to hide in? And that there are millions of books for us to swallow? It's an ink drinker's paradise!"

"Let's see first," Draculink grumbled.

"What's on the ground in front of the tower?" Carmilla asked. "It looks like trees."

"Those *are* trees, along with flowers and benches. It's the perfect garden for people in love," I said. "We'll be able to use our twin straw while the birds sing and the trees murmur in the wind."

My little girlfriend was under the place's spell. In her wide-open eyes, I was able to see fragments of blue sky. Draculink was more cautious.

"I fear the building is too modern for me," he said.

"Don't worry, Uncle. You'll be safe over there. And the giant library is less than a mile away from your old cemetery!"

This reassured him. He was not about to turn into dust. . . .

"In that case, let's go! This walk has made me unbelievably thirsty."

And, surprisingly, his pace accelerated!

We started exploring the tower, got lost a couple of times, and finally packed the three caskets into an elevator and pressed

32

the button for the top floor. But once the door opened . . .

"Aaaahhh!"

Hearing Carmilla's terrified scream, I rushed to her rescue. In my haste, I stumbled and the caskets piled on top of me. The next thing I saw was a pair of boots worn by a night watchman.

Carmilla was shaking like a leaf, but she managed to help me up. The guard was motionless and mute. What was he waiting for?

Draculink stared at him, looking petrified. Discreetly I started retreating toward an emergency staircase.

"Don't flee!" the guard said as I was about to run down the stairs. "I have a story to tell you. You'll find it quite entertaining."

He displayed a wide smile.

"My name is Serge. In the old days, I owned a bookstore. Once, a strange customer entered my shop. He was called . . . Draculink. Soon I had to sell my store, for I was consuming my books instead of selling them. But I have no regrets."

Uncle Draculink suddenly recognized Serge and chuckled.

"You can feel at home here," said the former bookstore owner. "You have unknowingly entered Dracuville, the city of ink drinkers. Come and have a look around our little kingdom."

I took Carmilla's hand and Uncle Draculink's and we followed Serge into the heart of the Library of the World.

Under the parking area was an extraordinary space that had been dug out by the ink

drinkers. And in front of our eyes, an underground cemetery oddly reminiscent of Uncle's was spread out before us. It was just a bit smaller, and lit by halogen lamps for lack of sun and moon.

Draculink bent down and grabbed a handful of mud. "But . . ."

"Yes, indeed," said Serge, "it is the very same mud as in your cemetery. We carried it here with buckets over several months. So you see, none of us risks drying up. We knew that one day or another, you would end up here."

I could tell that the old ink drinker was not totally happy yet. I muttered a few words into Carmilla's ear. Then we took off running.

"Where are you going?"

"We're going to bring back some wood. Your casket has to be repaired. You need some rest after all this turmoil."

We preferred not to wait for Uncle's reply, since he's not known for his sense of humor. And I had another project brewing, which only Carmilla knew about—and for good reason . . . I was planning to build a casket for two!

About the Author

Éric Sanvoisin is one bizarre writer. Using a straw, he loves to suck the ink from all the fan letters he receives. That's what inspired him to write all the ink drinker stories. In *The City of Ink Drinkers*, the giant library is actually the Bibliothèque Nationale, which can be found along the River Seine in Paris. Sanvoisin is sure that just as there are blood brothers and blood sisters, everyone who reads this book will become his ink brother or ink sister. If you write to him, he will send you a straw. That's a promise, or else he won't be writing again anytime soon.

About the Illustrator

MARTIN MATJE

is an illustrator